Dear Parent:

Congratulations! Your child is taking the first steps on an exciting journey. The destination? Independent reading!

STEP INTO READING® will help your child get there. The program offers books at five levels that accompany children from their first attempts at reading to reading success. Each step includes fun stories, fiction and nonfiction, and colorful art. There are also Step into Reading Sticker Books, Step into Reading Math Readers, and Step into Reading Phonics Readers— a complete literacy program with something to interest every child.

Learning to Read, Step by Step!

Ready to Read   Preschool–Kindergarten
• big type and easy words • rhyme and rhythm • picture clues
For children who know the alphabet and are eager to begin reading.

Reading with Help   Preschool–Grade 1
• basic vocabulary • short sentences • simple stories
For children who recognize familiar words and sound out new words with help.

Reading on Your Own   Grades 1–3
• engaging characters • easy-to-follow plots • popular topics
For children who are ready to read on their own.

Reading Paragraphs   Grades 2–3
• challenging vocabulary • short paragraphs • exciting stories
For newly independent readers who read simple sentences with confidence.

Ready for Chapters   Grades 2–4
• chapters • longer paragraphs • full-color art
For children who want to take the plunge into chapter books but still like colorful pictures.

STEP INTO READING® is designed to give every child a successful reading experience. The grade levels are only guides. Children can progress through the steps at their own speed, developing confidence in their reading, no matter what their grade.

Remember, a lifetime love of reading starts with a single step!

For Breylee and Rayna, with love
—J. L. W.

www.stepintoreading.com

Educators and librarians, for a variety of teaching tools, visit us at www.randomhouse.com/teachers

Library of Congress Cataloging-in-Publication Data
Weinberg, Jennifer, 1970–
Surprise for a princess / by Jennifer Liberts Weinberg.
    p. cm. — (Step into reading. Step 2 book)
SUMMARY: The fairies Flora, Fauna, and Merryweather make a mess trying to surprise Briar Rose on her birthday, but their magic fixes things in the end.
ISBN 0-7364-2132-7—ISBN 0-7364-8022-6 (lib. bdg. : alk. paper)
[1. Birthdays—Fiction. 2. Fairies—Fiction. 3. Magic—Fiction.] I. Title. II. Series.
PZ7.W436345 Su 2003 [E]—dc21 2002007447

Printed in the United States of America   10 9 8 7 6 5 4 3 2 1

STEP INTO READING, RANDOM HOUSE, and the Random House colophon are registered trademarks of Random House, Inc.

DISNEP
♦ PRINCESS

Surprise for a Princess

By Jennifer Liberts Weinberg
Illustrated by Peter Emslie
and Elisa Marrucchi

Random House 🏠 New York

Once upon a time there was a girl named Briar Rose.

She lived in
the forest with
three fairies.
Their names were
Flora, Fauna,
and Merryweather.

One day,
the fairies sent
Briar Rose out
to pick berries.

While she was gone,
they planned
a surprise.

"Let's have a party for Briar Rose," said Merryweather. "With a cake!" said Fauna.

"And a dress
fit for a princess,"
said Flora.

Flora began
to make the dress.

She cut.

She pinned.

She trimmed.

Merryweather tried
to help.
But the dress
was a mess.

There was too
much cloth.
And there were too
many bows.

"Oh, no!"
said Fauna.
"It is awful!"
said Merryweather.

Fauna began
to make the cake.
She read from
a cookbook.
It said she needed
eggs, flour,
and milk.

Fauna mixed.
And spilled.

And dribbled.
And dropped.

The milk dripped
onto the floor.
And the eggs
rolled off the table!
Crack!

At last the cake
was baked and iced.
But the icing slid
off the top.
And the candles
would not stand up.

"It is awful!"
said Merryweather.
"A flop!"
said Flora.

The fairies began
to worry.

Briar Rose was
coming home soon.

"I know just
the trick,"
said Merryweather.

She gave each fairy
a wand.
"Magic!"
they cried.
With a wave
of their wands . . .

26

Poof!

The cottage

was clean as

a whistle.

Poof!

The cake

was as pretty

as a picture.

Poof!
The dress
was fit
for a princess.

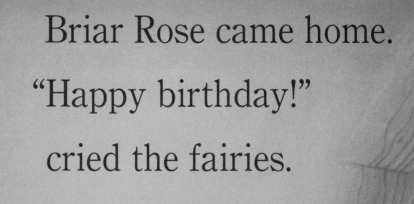

Briar Rose came home.
"Happy birthday!"
cried the fairies.

"Thank you!"
said Briar Rose.
"This is the
best surprise ever!"

The End